I0618242

SEEKING CATHERINE

JOSIE RIVIERA

Copyright 2012 by Josie Riviera

This book is a work of fiction and any resemblance to persons, living or dead, or places, events or locales is purely coincidental. The characters are the product of the author's imagination and used fictitiously.

Warning: The unauthorized reproduction or distribution of this copyrighted work is illegal. No part of this book may be scanned, uploaded or distributed via the Internet or any other means without the permission of the author. Please purchase only authorized editions and do not participate in the electronic piracy of copyrighted material. Thank you for respecting the hard work of the author.

Published in the United States of America

This book is dedicated to all my wonderful readers who have supported me every inch of the way.
THANK YOU!

CHAPTER 1

he Bankside, London, 1544

A PALE, midafternoon sun peeked through the ripped draperies of Hollands Leaguer, the most notorious brothel in all of England. Sitting in a downstairs study, Catherine Sudfield sipped her cup of blackberry wine and then swore in fluent French at the ledgers strewn across her desk.

Like the whore she'd become, she'd shed the respectability of her former life as the proper Mistress Catherine, eldest daughter of an earl.

Drinking and swearing were the least of her concerns.

She took another swig of wine and set down her cup. As she studied the ledgers, she willed the numbers to change. Normally the brothel turned a nightly profit, yet for the third consecutive day, earnings were suspiciously low.

The owner of the brothel, Sir Thomas Windchoice, was in nearby Dartford for the week, tending to his various corrupt businesses. When he returned and learned of the

1

income deficit, he would freely dispense accusations, blame, and … beatings.

To the women who worked at the brothel, of course. Never for the thieves who prowled the Bankside like scavengers, or the rich men who used and abused the whores for their pleasure.

Luckily, and she used the term loosely, she wasn't expected to amuse the long line of gentlemen who paid so exorbitantly for the prostitutes' favors.

Catherine's favors were for Sir Thomas's exclusive use.

She was fortunate. She had only one man to please.

One vile, despicable, merciless man.

The thought of Sir Thomas's sugar-coated mouth and sticky hands brought the usual shudder down her spine.

She shook it off.

With a spine-stiffening sigh, she picked up her feather quill and pulled her mind back to the uncooperative ledgers. She was a hardened woman after all, with an innate business sense and a determination to survive.

Interrupted by a man's low, insistent voice at the front entry, she peered through the doorway of her study. Bess, the brothel's elderly madam, unsuccessfully tried to deter a tall dark-haired man from making his way down the hallway.

"Sir, we are closed until eventide," Bess shouted, relying heavily on her cane as she hobbled after him. "The women are resting. If you wish to while away your afternoon hours until we reopen, enjoy a pot of ale at the Bear Gardens down the lane."

"Either you are deaf," came the terse reply, "or you refuse to listen. I abhor drunks and never liked bears. I am here to see a woman I have not seen in several years."

Dear heavens.

Catherine's entire body stiffened as she recognized the male voice.

Stefan Boswell. Her long-ago confidant. Her long-ago friend. Her long-ago love.

Surely, he couldn't have found her after all this time.

That same man, unannounced and certainly uninvited, was walking down the hall directly toward her study.

The feather quill fell from her hand. Her gasp, well past surprised, tightened her stomach. She pushed at the pins securing her wimple and stood, slowly, like a woman far older than her two and twenty years.

She smoothed her red satin gown, turned back the frayed white fur on the sleeves, and stood erect, trying to make her small frame seem taller. What did he want with her? She wouldn't give him the benefit of a direct confrontation. Should she wait for him to speak first?

Her hands shook as she clenched them to her sides.

Stefan stopped when he reached her study and leaned one shoulder against the doorframe, preventing her from darting past him. He was richly attired in a purple doublet, leather jerkin, and brocade gown, and he filled the room with his proud demeanor and the masculine air of fine horses and finer wool. A black ermine-trimmed cloak draped about his shoulders, giving him a regal appearance. Turning, he removed his broad-brimmed hat and handed it to a scowling Bess.

Then he spun back to Catherine and smiled. He stretched out his arms, his warm dark eyes trying to meet her gaze.

She wouldn't.

He waited for her to say something.

She didn't.

"Good day, my lady. 'Tis a pleasure to see you again," he said.

Catherine blinked hard at the recklessly good-looking male standing a few feet from her desk. The man who'd once pledged his love and then left her without a word of explanation. She gave a slight dip of her head and kept her feet rooted to the floor.

"Unfortunately, sir," she replied, "I cannot say the same."

Stefan's black brows lifted. His hands did the opposite.

He hadn't changed, she'd give him that. The boyish features of his youth had toughened, but his chin was still firm, his mouth set in a determined line. That familiar gaze, still trying to catch hers, held a coal-black, rakish gleam. And his face. Tanned and handsome. Affable and urbane. He'd always had such a mesmerizing, commanding face. But his expression wasn't as self-assured as she'd remembered, posing more questions than answers.

Bess pushed a graying wisp of hair beneath her close-fitting cap. "I could not stop the bloody scoundrel," she mouthed to Catherine.

Catherine nodded. She understood. There'd never been any dissuading Stefan, not when he set his mind on whatever goals danced in his head.

"A beautiful woman like you was not meant for this," he said.

He searched her face for one second too long and then his gaze traveled downward, resting on the square, low-cut neckline of her gaudy gown.

Her fingers fidgeted, itching to slap him across the face for his audacity. She wanted to wrench her bodice to her chin, and cursed herself for feeling so self-conscious. Instead, she kept her fists at her sides, trying to contain the emotions rising in her chest.

Surprise. Happiness. Fury. Surprise and happiness, though, had fled with his last remark. Only fury remained, lodged in the back of her throat, stopping her from taking a breath.

"What was I meant for?" she finally asked. "Are you trying to fix me? Mayhap change me back into a naïve girl?"

"Should I be? Fixing you?"

She almost said "Aye, you are the only person who can," but what was the point of a discussion about the past?

She swallowed. Neither of them spoke.

His gaze returned to her face and he didn't bother to hide his frown.

"You are apparently misguided in your choice of gowns," he said. "Has no one advised you on how a lady should properly dress?"

She winced from the stinging barb, the disparagement in his gaze. "I am dressed perfectly for an afternoon at Hollands Leaguer."

"Perfectly dressed for a whore, not a lady."

"Apparently, you are the same rake I remember," she shot back. "You are as callous as ever."

"'Tis not quite the welcome I expected."

"Nor the welcome you deserve," she retorted. "How did you manage to enter the brothel? The outer doors are locked to afternoon patrons."

"Gypsy magic," he quipped, coupling his explanation with an implacably cool gaze and ironic smile.

"You never believed in Gypsy superstitions or any type of luck, whether good or bad."

"I used to believe that people made their own luck and the rest is happenstance."

"Surely even the most jaded of us believe in God."

He half-laughed. "I always appreciated the way you finished my thoughts, provoking me to disagree. But this time you are correct. People make their own luck, but now I believe hard work is combined with fate, or, as you used to call it, divine intervention."

"How did you say you got in?" She shifted, clenching and unclenching her hands. "And why did you say you were here?"

"I have not said. Not yet, anyway."

She sighed and rubbed her temples. Most likely it was his noble authority laced with well-honed male charm that made him believe he was allowed entrance through her bolted door, or any bolted door, for that matter.

She glanced at him, at the man she remembered. Same fortitude in his expression. Same resolve in his stance. Same determination in his tone.

He kept his gaze on her. Thoughtful. Alert. Much too discerning. As if he had a lot to tell her, a lot of mistakes and secrets that had festered too long.

She shook her head. Thinking about the past was impractical. She was a no-nonsense woman who faced her adversities head-on. She couldn't dwell on circumstances that could never be changed.

"Shall we try our 'Good day' again, my lady?" he asked.

"There is no need for formal greetings. We have already said enough." She took several steps around her desk and headed for the doorway. Stefan still blocked her, but he was a minor deterrent. As soon as she made eye contact with Bess, they'd usher him out together. Surely, he was polite enough to leave quietly.

Before she walked halfway across the chamber, Stefan stepped forward, a slight hitch in his gait. Strange, she'd never known his strides to be anything less than strong and confident.

Before she could question him, he grabbed her forearms. "Where are you going?"

She tried to twist free, but failed. "I am not going anywhere because I live here. You, however, are leaving."

He kept his fingers firmly clamped on her arms. "Are you not the least bit curious as to why I am here?"

"For a quick tumble in a prostitute's bed?"

He frowned. "You can do better than that."

"Mayhap the gentleman wishes to pay for two women?" Bess, always the businesswoman, interjected from the hallway.

Catherine shot Bess an infuriated glare. "Do not give him any outrageous ideas. From what I remember, he has plenty of his own."

Stefan could not have looked more amused. "Along with some new ones."

A warm flush crept up her face as her gaze snapped back to his. Dear heavens, she couldn't believe his nonchalance.

"The more women you want, the more coin you pay," Bess said.

He flinched, slightly, but didn't turn, continuing to face Catherine.

"I want to watch," he said.

Catherine didn't mean to gasp aloud, but she did.

In the hallway, Bess nodded vigorously. Always, always the businesswoman. The degradations, the beatings, the abuse to the harlots, none of it mattered. Nothing except the money.

Catherine kept her breathing steady. "Stefan, the only watching you will do is watching me escort you out the front door."

His grin widened. "There you go again, finishing my sentences. I said I want to watch—"

"I do not give a pig's ear what you want to watch," she interrupted. "As long as 'tis somewhere else. Try watching and wagering on the bear-baiting down the lane." She spoke more rapidly with each breath, well aware she might soon be rambling, a terrible affliction that came over her whenever she was rattled.

"Bear-baiting was already suggested by your inhospitable madam as a way to get rid of me. As I explained, I did not walk across London Bridge to be entertained by bears."

Catherine resolutely refrained from asking what type of entertainment might interest him. She kept her gaze on the doorway and tried to sidestep him. His hands remained tight on her forearms.

"Let me pass," she warned.

"If I agree, can we talk amicably? I came a long way and my needs are simple."

I want to watch.

She shivered. She'd rather die than have Stefan watch the depraved Sir Thomas Windchoice when he visited her chamber, not for all the coin in England.

"Of course, we can speak amicably," she agreed, adding lying to her growing list of vices. She'd ask one of the other women to help throw him into the street as soon as she figured out a way past him.

He released his grip on her arms. "At least you have grown more amiable through the years. The younger, impetuous Catherine might have—"

"Complied?" Her fist had a mind of its own and caught Stefan squarely in the jaw. "That woman no longer exists."

CHAPTER 2

To his credit, Stefan didn't flinch nor finger the welt forming on his jaw. He muttered indistinguishable words in his foreign Gypsy language, reclaimed her forearms, and held firm. "You may need a few more years to soften."

She tightened her lips and struggled for control. "Try one hundred."

"Can you listen for one minute? 'Tis all the time I need."

"Then begin."

He lifted his hands, took a step backward and nodded in an oh-so-cordial manner. "You may speak first, darling."

Darling? He used to call her darling, a long time ago. She used to call him …

Briefly, she closed her eyes. Her heart squeezed with a caring she didn't want to feel. She almost took the bait and asked why he used the endearment now, after so many years had passed. She wasn't good at keeping questions to herself, so she laughed instead, albeit too loudly. That covered the pain.

But sadness had a way of resurfacing.

She blinked back unwelcome tears and inclined one hand toward the hallway. "You asked me to begin, so I shall. Listen carefully, for I do not need a full minute. I do not care what you do, what you say, what you watch, but your minute is over."

"Only twenty seconds has passed."

She answered him with a small nod. "Bess will show you the way out."

"On the contrary, I will show Bess out. She can try her hand at wagering on the wretched bears." Stefan walked the short distance to the door, effortlessly ushered Bess down the hallway whilst whispering in her ear, and then stepped back into the study, latching the door behind him.

His resolve was back, the expression set firmly on his face.

"My additional forty seconds begins now," he said.

CHAPTER 3

*D*espite herself, a smile curved the corners of Catherine's lips.

"How did you manage to persuade Bess to leave so quickly? She is fiercely protective of the women." Catherine held up a hand. "Let me guess. 'Tis your male—"

"Bribery." Solemnly, Stefan brandished a gold coin from his cloak. "All women listen to money."

"I am utterly impervious to bribery," she said quietly.

She was about to add that she was utterly impervious to him, but that was untrue. Besides, she'd already lied once.

Stefan didn't answer. Now that the initial surprise of seeing him had settled in her stomach like a dull ache, Catherine allowed the silence to roll between them.

He'd grown an appealing roughness she didn't recall from his younger days. That same black, silky hair fell straight across his forehead. The fine wool cloak stretched taut over his broad shoulders, a gold sash was laced at his slim waist. His shirt was open at his throat, exposing dark chest hair against the ruff's white neckline.

He grinned, a lazy grin. "Do I meet with your approval?"

She wanted to snap "Nay, you are dressed too fancy for a rake," but opted for truthfulness. After all, it was only a few minutes since lie number one.

"Aye," she said, but couldn't resist adding, "Although because I live at Hollands Leaguer, I am not at all particular these days."

Cool as a December afternoon, he ignored the backhanded compliment and seemed to bite back a smirk. "I will start over, for I forget my manners. Should I address you as Mistress Catherine or Catherine?"

"Mistress Catherine will do."

He laughed, deep and infectious. "And you can call me Stefan."

Stefan. Her Stefan.

Her smile came. She couldn't help it. "How could I ever forget you, Stefan?"

"If you had, my pride would have suffered quite a blow."

"Do not feign modesty, for you are Lord Boswell now, no longer the humble lad born of a Yorkshire blacksmith."

His father had been the town drunk, but Catherine didn't need to add that information. The younger Stefan had suffered enough under the cruel taunts of the local villagers. She might be eager to bring him down a nick or two, but not that eager nor that cruel.

He threw her the confident smile she well remembered, the one he used to disguise his vulnerability. "I am a proper baron now."

"All puffed-up as any I have seen. If rumors stand true, you are also one of the wealthiest landowners in England."

He said nothing, just nodded.

"On your own," she continued, "you climbed the ranks from soldier to lawyer to Privy Council, and you are welcomed in every aristocratic court in Europe."

"Are you granting an extension to my one-minute explanation to extol my virtues?" he asked.

"I am simply feeling generous."

He made no attempt to stifle his laugh. "You've kept a detailed account of my whereabouts, Mistress Catherine. My mood is steadily improving."

His mood might be improving, but hers was definitely deteriorating. He hadn't been interested enough to keep track of her, nor her hopeless life now gone wrong.

She exhaled a long, drawn-out breath and pressed on.

"Some say you are a personal friend of King Henry the VIII."

"Because I am the proverbial self-made gentleman at the age of eight and twenty."

"But we both know you are far from a gentleman."

The coal in his black eyes sparked. "My nobleness is tainted with a trace of Romany blood. No one knows my true heritage except you."

"The fact that you are a Gypsy matters naught. The man I remember bore no allegiance to heritage, nor family, nor the woman he left behind."

He stiffened, his lips drew together. "May I explain myself?"

"You are several years too late."

He nodded a touché and scanned the room, the worn-out draperies, the ostentatious red silk wallpaper, the brazen naked cherubs dancing across the ceiling in the most provocative of positions. After a beat too long, his gaze found hers again, but his eyes no longer held their previous warmth.

"'Twould appear you are no longer the inexperienced girl I once knew."

"I changed," she conceded.

"Mistress Catherine, you have become—"

"Successful."

What a word. Successful in what sense? That she had made a way for herself when no other way existed? That she was alive? That she'd survived? Aye, she was successful in that sense. As long as he didn't use the word 'whore.'

"I was going to say you are lovelier than I ever imagined."

She swallowed as unexpected tears welled. She was prepared for an attack on her character, a contemptuous snicker, a lecherous grin. But if Stefan spoke with kindness, her tenuous hold on her emotions would weaken and she would become a blubbering, pathetic fool.

But hadn't he always spoken kindly, treating her as if she were his most precious jewel?

Aye, when she was seventeen. Young. Unafraid. Optimistic. Wasn't that how life was supposed to work—before the realities of adulthood piled obligations on one's shoulders that refused to be abandoned?

She pulled her stance straighter. With a composure she didn't feel, she walked back to the safety of her desk and stood behind it, erect and composed.

It served as a wooden shield from him and his new lofty life.

He stayed where he was, in the middle of the chamber. He glanced at the ledgers on her desk and his black eyebrows drew together in a scowl.

She shuffled the parchment, trying to look busy, knowing the numbers waited for her attention.

"I was examining the ledgers before you arrived," she said, wondering why she felt pressed to explain. "The brothel has not turned a profit this week."

"Should I be concerned?" he asked blandly. "Is there a lack of salacious men prowling the Bankside?"

A sigh escaped before she could hide it. "When Sir

Thomas returns, he will force the prostitutes to work nonstop, pleasing a vast assortment of customers. To make up for the income loss, of course."

"One of these women better not be you." Stefan positively glowered. "And this Sir Thomas is—"

"Sir Thomas is the owner of Hollands Leaguer," she said, inwardly congratulating herself. She'd said his name with only the slightest shiver.

"'Tis enlightening that the reason you work at a brothel has little to do with money. Do you enjoy coupling with different men merely for pleasure and excitement?"

She froze, startled by Stefan's allegations disguised in a chilly but conversational tone. He still had the ability to control their discussion by swerving around an unexpected corner.

"I would never justify such a contemptuous question with an answer," she said.

"You were always such an innocent. Whatever happened?"

"I grew up."

He studied her intently, almost beseechingly. "All these years, I envisioned my saintly Catherine saving herself for when she saw me again. I thought I knew you so well."

She angrily swiped at the wetness at the corner of her eyes. "You saw what you wanted to see—a doting female who hung onto your every utterance."

He crossed the room with an uneven gait. "How many men do you entertain, Catherine?" Stefan's tone had turned silky, sending apprehension down her spine. And he no longer addressed her as 'Mistress Catherine.'

"Do you need a cane?" she asked, deflecting his question.

He appeared surprised, but quickly hid the expression with a bland smile. "Sometimes."

"Do you suffer from gout because of your fancy new life?"

"Gout? Me? Believe whatever you wish." He almost looked like he'd laugh aloud, although no sound crossed his lips. His large frame cast a looming shadow across her desk as he leaned forward. "How many men do you entertain, Catherine? I am asking a second time."

"I cannot believe you have the impudence—"

"How many?"

She folded her arms and listlessly stared at the doorframe behind him. "God curse you."

"God should. I probably deserve it. But I am entitled to know."

"You must be joking. You are entitled to nothing but the past, which no longer exists."

"The past and the present are intermingled."

"You are truly playing the part of a pompous nobleman. You wear the silk and brocade well." She wanted to say more, but the jibes stayed where they were, caught tight in her constricted throat. Stefan had been an incorrigible wastrel, but he'd always looked out for her safety and treated her with admiration and respect. Those were the days when it felt good to be a woman, when she was being courted by her shining, brave Gypsy knight.

He pressed nearer. "How many men?"

She tried to stall, but he leaned even closer.

She sucked in air. "One." She thought she might vomit. "Only one."

"Only one." His face blanched. He braced himself on the desk, his warm breath heating her face. "And how much do you charge this one lucky man? For me, your favors were free."

Her accusing glare wasn't lost on him, for he took a step back.

"You gave up all claim to me when you left Yorkshire without a word," she said.

"I am sorry for my past actions."

"Good. The matter is settled then. You apologized and all is forgiven."

His eyes narrowed. He glanced at the ledgers. "You are a woman who counts her coin. Do you charge this one man by the hour or the coupling?"

Her body's response to his deliberate degradation was an uncontrolled trembling and a nagging humiliation. Her mind was stricken by the inability to think at all. And both realizations gave way to an understanding she didn't want to acknowledge.

Stefan Boswell still had the power to hurt her, to bring up emotions long buried in a tiny, safe compartment in her heart. There the memories had sat, tucked away, frozen in time.

Like the remembrance of the summer of her seventeenth year, and the way they'd laughed together, run barefoot through the fields together, made plans for their future together.

Her chest ached, her body felt cold. Aye, that tiny compartment was the best

place, the only place, because she still cared for him. Cared? She shook her head. What a mild word. After five long years, she still loved him, wanted him to look at her with the same approval, wanted to hear his unrestrained, deep laugh.

She lifted her chin, nice and high. The younger, unsophisticated Catherine would have buckled under his steady gaze, asked forgiveness for becoming a loose woman. The mature, wiser Catherine had learned a bitter lesson, one that the whores had taught her about a man's true nature. Men wanted utmost authority. Women were little more than chattel.

She could hardly fathom the power Stefan would wield over her if he knew how much she cherished the memories of their lost love.

She summoned all the haughtiness she could in order to utter her greatest lie. "My services are far from free. Indeed, I doubt even a man as affluent as you could afford me. I am no longer the girl of seventeen who offered herself to an older man merely because she was infatuated by his flowery words and false promises."

"Be fair, Catherine. I never promised I would remain in Yorkshire forever."

She shook her head. "You owe me no explanation for leaving. 'Tis what Gypsies do best. They roam."

"I was tempted beyond distraction by you. I debated and argued with myself.

Should I stay—should I depart." His voice lowered. "You will never know how much I regret leaving you."

"You disappeared from all our lives, not just mine. Your family, your friends, no one knew where you had gone. Then a couple of years ago, the villagers began talking about your successes. 'Twas as if you'd reappeared after a long visit abroad."

He shrugged and then stood very still.

When he remained silent with no explanation, she said softly, "Some wondered why you never returned to Yorkshire, although the rumors placed you in London. The year I left for the Bankside, your whereabouts were still uncertain."

"I had to leave Yorkshire. You had said yourself that you despised the despair, the poverty. You knew I sought adventure and wanted a new life, a better life. I feared I would become content with very little, and end up as apathetic as my father."

Content with me, Catherine wanted to shout, Was that so little? Was that so frightening? But she didn't shout. In fact, she hardly raised her tone.

"'Tis time to return to your successful life in London, my lord."

"I like it better when you call me Stefan."

"Go whilst we are still able to speak civilly to each other. A minute has passed tenfold. This brothel is indeed closed."

"You never closed yourself to me before. Once, I knew your every thought." His voice was husky, the timbre rich and meaningful. And oh-so-familiar.

His eyes darkened to pitch-black. All sin. All pleasure. All danger.

She braced her fingers on the desk to steady herself. Her legs were turning to silt just when she needed them most, and it took all of her effort to remain standing.

"What could you possibly want after all these years?" she asked.

There. The words came out, but they were shaky and too high-pitched. Had he noticed? She glanced up at him. His smile was meaningful. He had.

She expelled her breath in frustration and waited for him to speak.

He rewarded her with more silence. He'd become very skilled at that.

"Mayhap," she said, "you are jaded and require more outrageous amusement, but you will not find what you are looking for at the Bankside."

"This is the perfect place for me." His eyebrows rose in a sardonic curve. "I want to watch you, Mistress Catherine. Only you. Every day. Every hour. I want to watch you renounce this degrading life and walk out the door with me."

She was so relieved she reared back, trying to recall those blissful adolescent memories. But her mind wouldn't cooperate, preferring to focus on the naked cherubs dancing on the ceiling.

"And where shall we walk? To the center of London mayhap?" Somehow, she managed to keep her voice from shaking. "Shall I become your exclusive courtesan in an extravagant townhouse near Whitehall Palace?"

"I shall take you any way you will come."

"Unfortunately, you are several years too late."

She folded her hands together at her waist. Her nails dug into her palms as she considered the man to whom she'd once pledged her love. His handsome, angular features and the ever-present invitation in his gaze proved more forceful than she'd remembered. Even in his casual stance, he exuded a vigorous, persuasive strength.

His gaze assessed her, although his expression remained an impenetrable mask.

"Go to your chamber and pack your trunks."

In her past life, the life of her daydreams, she might have thrown herself into his arms and then scurried up the stairs to do whatever he commanded. But this was her life now. All her possessions were owned by Sir Thomas Windchoice, including her. Two years ago, she'd been sold to Sir Thomas by her greedy merchant uncle, because she was a hungry, worthless woman who needed to be clothed and fed. With both parents dead, she and her younger sister, Anne, were orphans. Catherine's sole use to her uncle was the coin he had received when she came to the Bankside. In return, he'd assured Catherine that her sister would be safe.

So now she was a piece of soiled goods, although once she'd enjoyed the life of a gently-reared, refined girl. Reality made her heart heavy and her lips quiver. She fixed her gaze on the ever-dancing cherubs. "I shall never return to Yorkshire."

"Catherine, a fine woman like you does not belong in a brothel."

Her stubborn pride had made her resilient and she had added mettle and temerity to her list of admirable traits. "Are you trying to save my reputation for some noble cause?"

"You are precious, yet you grant favors as a common whore, like a Winchester goose."

This was all wrong. She'd never imagined seeing Stefan again, certainly never thought he'd find her in a place like this. She should say something, give a plausible, indignant explanation to calm his angry, hurtful words. Something sophisticated, flippant, reassuring. Something to ease the confusion and regret on his face.

"I am not so common," she said. "I have survived great misfortunes and am still standing."

"You are my beautiful Catherine." Swiftly, he reached across the desk and pulled the pins from her wimple, along with the embroidered gold net securing her hair. His long fingers skimmed the tattered lace of her corset as he set the wimple and net on the desk. Her blonde hair spilled across her shoulders and down her back.

She retreated a step. Or was it two? The satin hem of her gown rustled along the wood floor.

"If you want my favors," she said, "you must pay for them."

She saw no annoyance in his face. In fact, his expression softened. "The Catherine I knew desired no payment. The Catherine I see beneath the painted lips and tantalizing gown is the innocent Catherine of my youth."

She was too busy trying to breathe, let alone reply. She shook her head in protest and tossed him a self-assured smile she didn't feel.

"Nay," she whispered. "She is gone."

"She is here," he said, his voice just as soft. "She stands courageously in front of me."

She studied this compelling man. His white linen shirt couldn't disguise the hard-muscles of his arms, which belied his position as a nobleman. The faint outline of a stubbly black beard shaded his resolute chin. Even now, after all these years, he was the handsomest man she'd ever seen.

"Please come home with me," he said.

"I have no home."

"We both have a home in Yorkshire, where we played as children."

"Children play. Adults move on to other pastimes."

His eyes flared, a sure sign that he was tiring of her verbal games.

He'd never been a patient man, preferring to seek his fortune in another town, another place, rather than waiting for fortune to come to him.

He studied the ledgers again on her desk and attempted a blasé shrug. "Is one of your pastimes keeping an account of your adventures?"

"I told you. I keep the books for Sir Thomas."

"Not anymore." He scooped up the ledgers, balled them into a fist, and tossed them to the floor.

She glanced down at them and then back at him. "What do you mean?"

"I mean that surely you recall the warm summer afternoons we used to spend together?"

Her heart stopped for a beat. He meant that their shared memories were still a part of him, mayhap hidden away in a same secret compartment like hers. He meant that the plans they'd once made were more than empty words whispered in a moment of first love.

She squeezed her eyes shut.

He meant that he still remembered their times together, and took pleasure in them.

But then he'd disappeared.

She opened her eyes. "They prove a credulous lack of judgment in my inexperienced youth."

"Gypsy magic was in the air. Could you feel it? Taste it?" His gaze lingered on her mouth. He bent halfway across her desk and cupped her face gently in his hands. "Darling, do you remember our first kiss?"

CHAPTER 4

*S*tefan wasn't prepared for the cup of blackberry wine that Catherine flung at him. He swerved to the side a second too late, adding a curse in colorful Romany. Though always on his guard, his gaze had been fixed on her provocative lips and not the dangerous flames leaping in her emerald eyes. He'd always lost his ability to think reasonably, and react quickly, when Catherine was near. Why should five lost years make any difference?

Methodically, he flicked the droplets of crimson wine from his black cloak. "I did not expect the mention of one pleasant kiss to cause quite this reaction."

She was staring straight ahead at a spot somewhere past him. Her arm raised, she still clutched the empty cup. Her breathing was shallow and quick, the upper swell of her breasts rising above her lacy bodice in an alluring display. A fabric girdle cinched her waist, and the cone-shaped skirt accentuated her slimness. She looked every inch the furious temptress.

He couldn't resist goading her. "'Twas a wonderful kiss, if

my memory serves me correctly. Apparently, you feel the same."

"Stefan, I attempted politeness." Fury vibrated through her voice. "I agreed to listen to your one-minute explanation. But now—"

"Now I have rendered you speechless?"

Her expression changed to one mark short of murder. She gathered what sounded like a bottomless breath. Apparently, she hadn't appreciated his teasing question.

Her slim fingers tensed around the cup. "You would be delighted if I were speechless, because then you could serenade me with your one-minute untruths. Mayhap I should grovel on my knees and beg for your forgiveness for my numerous offenses, whether real or imagined?"

He threw her his best wicked grin. "If you wish."

She lifted the cup over her head and took aim, a not-so-subtle hint, he decided, that he gentle his approach. He held up both hands in surrender.

"If I vow not to speak of kissing, will you vow not to shatter a perfectly good cup? You mentioned the brothel had not made a profit this week. You must watch every shilling."

"Get out. I shall never forgive you for coming here today and distressing me."

"I shall risk your continued distress, for I plan to return every day until I have convinced you to depart with me." As casually as he could, he reached across the desk and took the cup from her hand, setting it safely beyond her grasp.

She drew herself straight. She'd always done that whilst she composed herself, even as a young girl when she'd had to fend for herself and her sister whenever their sickly parents fell ill with fever.

"If you return, I shall summon the sheriff," she said, a tad too bravely.

"The dishonest sheriff who beds a different woman every

night? That sheriff?" Stefan gave a wry laugh. "I break no law for entering a brothel in the middle of the day. Besides, the sheriff and aldermen do not patrol the Bankside. This area is under the Bishop of Winchester's jurisdiction. And we both know the bishop does not care about his Winchester geese unless he plans to top one."

Catherine's delicate eyebrows drew together as her hands squeezed into fists. "You speak disrespectfully of honorable and holy men, as if they would be of no assistance to unprotected working women."

"Women like you?" he asked.

Her gaze fell, but not before he saw the helplessness across her features. He peered at the closed velvet draperies blocking out the sunlight as well as the filth of the streets, the bloodthirsty sports, and the knaves who lurked in the shadows of the lanes.

Stefan walked to the window. He tried to favor his bad leg, but had to bite back a pain-filled groan when he stepped too hard. He did not want her to know about the agony he'd endured in an Italian prison. He wanted, needed, her heart. Not her sympathy.

Parting the draperies, he eyed the gray dampness of the late October afternoon. The excrement from dirty chamber pots overflowed the gullies.

"Respectable London townspeople are grateful that the Thames separates them from the Bankside," he said quietly. "Is there a man who safeguards the women in this brothel?"

"No one you would know."

Her non-explanation screamed volumes, a call for help. Nonetheless she seemed to want him to believe she was unafraid.

"Is there anyone who protects you?" he asked.

He didn't expect an answer, and didn't get one.

Mayhap she tried to protect the prostitutes from the cruel

discipline of their master. Or, Stefan realized with a sick feeling in his gut, mayhap she was trying to protect herself. From him.

Go slow. Speak softly. Don't press too hard.

She might be afraid to trust him.

With good reason, his conscience reminded him. He'd abandoned her whilst his aspirations were high, foolishly enlisting in an English army without telling anyone. Wanting to come back to her as a hero because he'd gained King Henry's favor.

Instead, he had fought in a losing war.

"I know many influential people," he said. "They will help you."

"You are too late."

"I came back as soon as I was able." He knew his pitch was hollow as the horrible memories of battle pelted him, but it was all he could offer. He'd aspired to success and wealth for her, and, ironically, he'd lost her in the process. Because he'd believed she deserved more than what a poor lad from York-shire could offer.

He turned to her. She was skittish, a trapped deer, eyes glinting a combination of anguish and wariness.

"I am fortunate," he said lightly, "you did not have an entire jug of wine at your disposal or my hose would have been ruined along with my cloak."

He expected a smile from her, or at least an effort at a smile. Instead she stayed out of his reach. She eyed the empty cup on her desk and sighed wistfully. "'Twould have been a deplorable waste of an excellent wine."

"You have acquired a taste for wine?"

"Somewhere along my fallen path, I discovered wine is much more calming than mead."

So, this was the life she knew, the life of a harlot. A life full of drunkenness, bawdy men, and the indifferent exchange of coins.

He eyed the sweetness of her beauty, the demureness of her smile.

The Catherine he knew was no harlot.

"Please accept my apologies for my earlier questions and insinuations," he began.

"Accepted," she replied with admirable grace. There was that straight back again.

Accepted but not forgiven.

A muscle throbbed in his jaw. He was standing in a brothel for God's sake. She should be asking for his forgiveness. Finding her in such a seductive place, a place where women sold their bodies to men, added a little too much fire to his already burgeoning frustration and righteously-burning anger. The sharp pang of jealousy that jabbed each time he imagined her in another man's arms worsened his aggravation.

Moving quickly, he strode around the desk and caught her waist before she could slip from his hold. "You are coming with me. You will do as I say."

She twisted in his grasp and tore her gaze from his. "I do not comply with an errant man's demands, especially when his demands are delivered so coldly."

"I could warm you nicely."

She swallowed and squeezed her eyes closed. "I have grown accustomed to being cold."

"Living in a brothel, I assume you have learned seductive ways to keep a man warm."

"Your assumptions are incorrect." She opened her eyes and lifted her chin. "If anyone was the seducer in our past relationship, 'twas you, not me."

His gaze drifted over her perfect features. "When we

made plans for our wedding night, you promised that you would untie the strings on my codpiece and seduce me."

Just the thought of their wedding night had his body stirring with excitement.

"A million years ago." Fury blazed across her face. "Untie your own blasted codpiece."

"If you studied me more closely when I entered, you would have noticed I did not wear a codpiece today."

"I did not look at you ... there. 'Tis unfortunate you did not tie the codpiece around your throat."

A loud tap at the door made him spin round.

"Mistress Catherine?" a woman called.

"'Tis Bess," Catherine whispered.

"The ladies are waking from their naps and dressing," Bess shouted through the door. "Some wish to keep their breasts bare whilst they entertain the men at supper."

"'Excellent idea, Bess," Catherine called back.

"I am preparing a lamb stew. For dessert, we shall serve gingerbread."

Stefan's eyes widened as he turned back to Catherine. "Does this manner of dining include you?"

"Do you not enjoy gingerbread?" Catherine asked, pretending not to understand.

He shook his head to clear the sensual visions floating through his brain. "Tell Bess 'nay' to the breasts and 'aye' to the gingerbread."

"Tell her yourself. Just offer her more coin. You are adept at bribery."

He swallowed. His mouth was dry. Still the sensual visions.

"Actually, anyone with a shilling could bribe Bess," he said.

At least he could actually speak.

"I must unlatch the door, and you must leave," Catherine said.

"Not until you give your word that you will behave yourself this evening."

"Thomas will kill any man who dallies with me. I shall explain to Bess that you are my ... cousin, which gives us an explanation if Thomas starts asking questions about you."

"Will Bess believe you?"

"I hope that she will. I have known her for years, but I do not trust her. She feigns loyalty to me, but acts completely different when Thomas is around."

Stefan let go of Catherine's waist. As she started to the door, his hands captured hers.

"We have several unfinished matters, Mistress Catherine. And remember, tonight you will eat gingerbread fully clothed."

CHAPTER 5

*T*hree days. Seventy-two hours. Not long for a man who'd spent years in prison. But for Stefan, seventy-two hours felt like a decade.

He strode past the Bishop of Winchester's palace, the gruesome prison on Clink Street. Numerous actors idled about the theaters as he made his way to Hollands Leaguer. The afternoon promised a continuous gray drizzle, and his leather boots sloshed through the muddy streets.

Unwashed harlots slouched on the curbs, plying their trade. He shook his head at their offers and walked on, as brisk as his gait allowed. The dampness of the day reached his bones, the stench of urine assaulted his nostrils. He turned the ermine fur of his cloak up to his chin and continued past a row of run-down whorehouses.

Several minutes later he gave two abrupt raps on the locked door of Catherine's brothel, bringing Bess to the entrance.

"You missed the midday dinner," she said. "'Tis half past two o'clock."

"I enjoyed my curdled meal at the filthy tavern down the

lane," he replied. He stamped the mud from his boots as he entered the brothel, removed his broad-brimmed hat, and set his cane and hat in the entryway. Smiling, he offered Bess a gold coin. "I am here to see my ... cousin, Catherine Sudfield."

He couldn't offer any additional information on how he and his newly inherited cousin were related, and hoped that Bess wouldn't ask. Thankfully, she didn't. She did, however, inspect him from head to toe, frowning all the while. Clearly, he lacked something. Mayhap an additional gold coin or two.

"If Mistress Catherine be your cousin, then I be a horse's arse," Bess muttered as she led him up a flight of steep wooden stairs. After gesturing to a closed chamber door, she stuffed the gold coin into the front of her square bodice and lumbered down the stairs.

Catherine opened her door before Stefan knocked. He couldn't remember a time when she hadn't sensed his arrival well before he actually arrived. Call it a connection, call it a bond. Call it love.

Love. The word squeezed his heart.

"I returned as promised," he said.

Brilliant, he thought, just brilliant. Stefan Boswell, the man with all the right words at the wrong times.

Catherine, the object of his affection, sighed audibly and crossed her arms at her waist. Her eyes didn't shine with warmth because she was scowling at him. These weren't encouraging signs, but he'd never been a man to back down. And, he wanted Catherine very, very badly. He'd spent the past five years thinking only of her, clinging to the memory of her kind face to carry him through the hard years in prison.

Several golden strands of hair hung in loose waves around her shoulders, with the rest secured at the crown. Without paint on her face, the dark smudges beneath her eyes made her appear younger, like a child who'd been allowed to stay up past her bedtime too many nights in a row.

"Go away," she said.

"You really must learn to work on your greetings. 'Tis proper to say good day first."

She tried to close the door on him. "Good day. And go away."

She'd grown into quite the spitfire, with her flashing green eyes and that stinging bite to her tone. Still, he had to reach her, had to reach through her understandable anger, had to make her understand why he'd disappeared.

He stood firm in the doorway. "Please. I have so many regrets."

"The past is gone. Only the present is important."

"I am your past. I am your present."

I am your future.

But he didn't say those words aloud.

"May I come in?" he asked. "You know me well enough. I do not give up easily."

To his surprise, she laughed. "By all means. 'Twill take more effort to deter you."

Stefan stepped inside and closed the door, throwing the latch. Her chamber was surprisingly small and dimly lit by a low, flickering fire in the grate. One ragged curtain hanging over the arched window kept out the world. Her wooden bed was neatly made and pushed against the far wall. A rosewood bureau stood to the side of the bed holding a single lit candle.

The scents of sweet lavender and blackberry wine danced to his nostrils and he inhaled deeply.

"Did you miss me these past few days?" he asked.

She dropped her gaze, watching as her fingers rubbed the pleats of her gown. "When two days passed, I assumed you had returned to Yorkshire."

He replied noncommittally. "The reason I did not return sooner was because I was forced to attend to unexpected business matters."

"If you had waited any longer, I would not have been able to let you in. Sir Thomas is expected back within a day or so. I assure you, he is one person you will not want to meet."

"Good to know." Stefan carefully kept his voice detached. He grabbed Catherine's restless, cold hands in his warm ones. "I have a proposition for you, darling."

Her back stiffened.

"You want me to be your courtesan," she said dully.

"We were always well-suited."

Along with errant tears, anger spilled from her gaze. "Your faulty remembrances. Your faulty assumptions."

"'Tis a more lucrative lot than your current one," he said. "I will provide you with an elaborate home, lavish jewels, and servants who will attend to your every whim."

"And in return you will want?"

"The exclusive use of your body whenever I wish."

She wrenched her hands from his. "You describe my existing arrangement."

The small fire sputtering in the grate cast a reddish glow on her creamy complexion. Her features were delicate, her lips, sensuous and coral, beckoned him.

He slipped his fingers into the tendrils framing her face. "Does your current arrangement include the joy we once shared? Our Gypsy magic?"

Her whole body tensed. "'Tis but a memory. A good memory, but 'twill fade in time."

"How can you say our love will fade, knowing what we once shared?"

She shrugged, feigning a disinterest he knew she didn't feel. "The longer you stay, the more you place us both in danger."

"Danger from whom? The infamous Thomas Wind-choice? You said 'tis two days before he returns. Should I be frightened of him?"

She sighed and looked away. Those restless fingers again, rubbing the pleats of her worn gown.

Stefan cupped her face in his hands. "Confide in me so I can help you."

"Heed my advice and leave this wretched place."

"Not until I get some answers."

"Take your hands off me."

He didn't comply. For someone so undaunted she resembled a frightened doe, eyes wide, feet frozen in one place. Tears flowed freely now in a steady stream. She wiped her tears. They still flowed.

"You shall not win against someone as powerful as Sir Thomas. I have tried."

"I am powerful, too, Catherine. I am not the impoverished young man of our youth." He smoothed back those loose tendrils and tenderly kissed her forehead.

She drew a long, agitated breath. "You do not know him as well as I do."

Stefan tensed, but only for a beat. "No one will harm you when I am near."

"Sir Thomas is evil."

"Tell me about him."

Her features seemed to crumble. "He will force my sister into prostitution," she whispered, so softly that Stefan leaned closer.

"Anne? She cannot be older than a child."

"She is twelve years old." Sorrow flickered in Catherine's gaze. "And I will kill

anyone who threatens to harm her."

"My brave, sweet girl." Stefan spoke with a calmness he didn't feel. "You do not have to fight this battle alone. I will not allow anyone to ever hurt you or your family." He brushed his fingers across her tear-stained cheeks, and then hugged her to his chest. Her sobs, wrenched from deep inside her, drove a hole through his gut.

"Stefan." She raised tear-filled eyes to his. "I am so frightened."

"I will protect you."

"The last time I needed help, you disappeared."

He pulled back a hairsbreadth. Wasn't she right? Wasn't she always right? She was the practical person, seeing a situation for what it was, not mincing words. But she was warm and soft and fragile, and his desire to look after her overrode everything else.

He sighed and wrapped his arms tightly around her. "If I had known … "

If he had known, he never would have left, no matter how many fortunes awaited him.

"Today we will give up this wretched place," he said.

She didn't answer, just stared into his eyes and raised her chin.

Her expression was resolute. The tears had stopped.

"This is my home, and you must obey my commands. Today you will depart. Alone, and without me."

CHAPTER 6

*R*efusal did not sit well with most men and Stefan was no exception. He drew a steady breath into his lungs and let it out slowly.

"No one can force you to stay in a brothel. For God's sake, Catherine, you are mine."

With a sense of terrible premonition, he watched her spine straighten. Instinctively he loosened his hold and she stepped back, adjusting the fabric of her frayed satin gown.

"I belong to Sir Thomas Windchoice."

"You belong to me."

"Stefan, I am bound to him by a lawful agreement that cannot be broken, lest I wish my sister to be hauled to debtor's prison. Her body would be used up before she came of marriageable age."

"You are giving up your life for hers? Do not be a martyr, Catherine. I refuse to lose you to a cause you cannot win."

"There are girls working along the Bankside who are as young as ten years old. I cannot allow my regrettable fate to happen to my sister. Would you not do the same for your family?"

"Not if it meant sacrificing the woman I … "

There it was again. That unexpected tug on his heart, that sharp pang in his gut, that bellowing of a thousand emotions that came down to one word.

Love.

Blind, impetuous, mindless love.

"You were forced to give your body to another, but your heart belongs to me," he said.

Her lips formed an unyielding, stubborn line. "You have no claim on me."

"You are in love with Sir Thomas?"

She laughed, cool, piercingly brittle. "No one speaks of love at the Bankside. Men enjoy their favors and women feign bliss and take the drunken fools' coins."

Stefan's own smile was cold at her dismissive description of a harlot's life.

"But you love me," he said.

He had always considered himself persuasive, especially when stating the obvious. Or so he hoped, for he found himself holding his breath for her response.

Softly, she cleared her throat. "Once, I fancied I was in love with you. Once. But we were never betrothed."

"We had no signatures, but our fate was sealed with a kiss and an understanding." His tone was reduced to an edgy declaration. And his feet were planted in the middle of her chamber, when they should have been taking him to her side.

"You are confusing my heritage with yours," she said, "for I am not a Gypsy fortune teller. I have no tricks and read no palms. I work in a brothel. I am soiled and dirty. Most people would say I belong to many men."

Stefan wanted to assure her, using his best blithe banter, that all was forgiven. It wouldn't matter how many men had bedded her. Like the benevolent lord of his lands, he would pardon her past mistakes. He only cared about the present.

Because he loved her.

He looked around the shabby chamber. So now what should he do?

He searched his mind for a way to declare his love, but his gaze kept straying to her gleaming blonde hair. So many years ago, she'd straddled his bare chest and laughingly trailed her hair along his face, his mouth. They had lain on the ground, the grass sticking to their sweaty skin. His loins tightened at the memory of the fine, glossy texture of her hair. He dragged in a breath, imagining the intoxicating scent of pink and white roses, fresh summer grass, and the heat of a sultry afternoon.

He transferred his weight from one foot to the other and scrutinized her flawless features—her deep-set green eyes, which had narrowed suspiciously below elegant, arched brows. With a glower like that, she certainly wasn't offering undying love.

"Stop staring at me," she said.

"Am I staring?"

"You look as if you plan to devour me whole."

"Are you offering?"

She shook her head vigorously.

Aye, he was staring. Because her skin was the color of perfect porcelain, and her womanly body resembled the voluptuous curves of Venus. And because he'd tried his entire life to make her proud of him. Him, the poor lad born to the town drunks.

He glanced at her rebellious expression. "You are a fragile, beguiling picture."

A glorious blush of pink stained her cheeks. Her spiky brown lashes lowered, effectively shadowing her thoughts. "I am not so fragile anymore, Stefan."

He stroked his thumbs down the sides of her face. "I fear I shall speak the wrong words and you shall grab your skirts and dash from the room. Or you will vanish altogether, and I shall never find you no matter how frantically I search."

"You searched for me?"

"My most zealous investigators could not find you for over a year. All this time, you breathed the same London air as I, but resided in a place I never dreamed."

With implacable certainty, he added, "I needed you desperately, Catherine. I always have."

She squeezed her eyes shut for a second but thankfully, she didn't draw away. She seemed to struggle to keep her expression neutral.

His hands glided down her shoulders and rested on the curve of her waist. He kissed her forehead, the tip of her nose. He'd always liked doing that.

Emboldened, he added, "I intend to kiss you for the remainder of the afternoon."

"'Tis a lovely offer. Sadly, I must refuse."

"Your refusal is simply a challenge to me."

Her gaze glared defiance. "Call it whatever you wish."

"When have you ever known me to back down from a challenge?" He pulled her body close, such a delectable mold to his, and rested his hands on the small of her back. "You give me no choice but to change your mind. You know I like to win."

"We are not in our youth anymore, trying to outrun each other, wagering who can throw a stick the farthest across a stream. You—"

He caught her protest in a kiss.

"Stefan," she murmured. "We can never be."

He lifted his lips, just an inch. "Of course we can." He regarded her beautiful face just before his mouth met hers again. "Admit we belong together."

"Until you leave me again?" Her forehead puckered. Her

eyes implored him to say more, to finish her question with a hopeful response.

Before her circle of doubts and fears could intrude, he said, "I shall never abandon you. I love you."

She stilled for a moment, her expression clouding. "You love me?"

"I have always loved you."

She stood on her toes and twined her fingers around his nape. Her lips parted and she accepted his kiss.

"See how easy 'tis to kiss me?" he whispered.

"You are trying to persuade me to leave with you."

"Am I succeeding?"

She turned her head and his lips brushed her cheek.

She laughed. "You are quite successful if your goal is to miss my mouth. Alas, you will require a quizzing glass if your aim does not improve."

He swallowed her laugh with his lips. "We shall grow old together."

She melted against him. He felt her welcome his tongue whilst she offered hers in return. His lips wandered to her throat. One hand tugged on her bodice and linen chemise.

She shook her head. "Not here. Someone may find us."

He kept her body firmly curved against his and grinned. "Need I remind you that we are in a brothel?"

The heady, musky fragrance of her skin, the fresh, sweet scent of lavender, the tart blackberry wine on her tongue, combined like a powerful aphrodisiac.

He deepened his kiss. She was the one. She'd always been the one.

She groaned, a soft submission, and he guided her against the wall. With one hand, he caged her wrists over her head. He clamped his other arm possessively around her back, holding her captive.

"You are leaving with me."

She squirmed. "Blast you, Stefan, for being so persuasive."

His quiet laughter rang through the chamber. "Words of love."

CHAPTER 7

$\mathcal{C}$ atherine's chamber slanted as Stefan lifted her to her bed. Her gown twisted around her thighs and exposed her naked legs. She wore neither linen drawers nor stays. Obviously he'd noticed, for his gaze was positively voracious.

"Take your hair down, darling," he instructed as he strung unhurried kisses down her throat.

She removed the half dozen pins at her crown. Swiveling, she dropped the pins on the bureau near her bed. Her long hair tumbled over her shoulders.

When she swung back, Stefan had unlaced his cloak and flung it to the floor. His doublet and jerkin followed. She stared up at his chiseled face as he stood over her. A purposeful gleam shone in his black Gypsy eyes. His linen shirt hung past his thighs, outlining his codpiece and striped hose. He lifted a sardonic eyebrow, and she bit back a baiting comment concerning codpieces—his in particular.

Her magnificent Stefan. Her valiant Gypsy knight. Her strong protector.

He wanted her, and she wanted him. He said he loved her,

and she loved him. And her heart knew she'd already forgiven him for abandoning her all those years ago.

"Catherine," he whispered in a husky tone. "'Tis been so long."

She reached out her arms to welcome him. "I missed you."

The bed sank under his weight as he lowered his body beside hers. The chilly air against her bare legs sent a tremor through her body.

He covered them both with the bed linens. Then he joined his mouth to hers, his kisses feathery light and maddeningly restrained. He was a man who liked to kiss. He had told her that once, although he hadn't needed to. She'd known by the way he kissed—intent, raw, tormenting.

When he raised his head, his breathing came rough.

"From this day, promise me that I am the only man who will share your bed." His fingers skipped impatiently along her hips. "Promise me."

She stared into his eyes, molten with love. "When Sir Thomas finds you, he will kill you. His wrath is fearful. He will seek revenge any vindictive way he can."

"I assure you, he shan't find me, nor kill me. Nor will he harm you."

"How do you know this?"

"Because I found him. Be assured that he was most agreeable to my terms."

"Terms? What terms?"

"Thomas Windchoice has released you from your agreement."

She rubbed her face with her hands. "He would never consent. Sir Thomas—"

"Sir Thomas be damned, Catherine." Stefan sat up and tried to quell her uncertainty with a reassuring smile. "He will not be seeing the shores of England for some good many years, for he is taking an extended journey to Italy."

A sob escaped her mouth. She clamped a fist to her lips and attempted to contain the wave of relief sweeping through her.

"Are you certain?" she asked.

"Impeccably certain."

"How did you persuade him?"

"A man I once considered my enemy found that 'twas more lucrative to become my friend." Stefan dried the tears on her lashes with a kiss. "Sir Thomas has used women for the last time."

She sat up beside him. "And who is this friend?"

Stefan smiled. "Gypsies have roamed Europe for many years."

"That does not answer my question in the slightest. You truly are the most exasperating man." Her fingers quivered, restless to touch the taut skin beneath his linen shirt.

"Before we spoke of Sir Thomas's travels and my new-found friend, I believe we were speaking about promises to be made."

"I promise you will be the only man to share my bed if you promise to do something for me," she said.

He laughed. "There are conditions?"

"You must promise to continue to kiss me."

In the muted light of the low, sparking fire, the last emotion Catherine had expected to see in Stefan's expression was indecision. She licked her lips and pressed them together, waiting for his good-natured laugh to return.

He hesitated a moment too long. And then, slowly, he shrugged off his shirt.

She blinked, noticing for the first time the jagged scars etched across his chest. "Dear heavens." She bolted upright. Her fingers grazed the angriest gash. "Whatever happened?" Her voice quivered with concern for him, along with wariness and uncertainty.

Stefan's gaze stayed on her face. "I fought a war in the south of England for King Henry. Afterward, I spent two years rotting in an Italian prison."

Her fingers lightly touched the springy black hair on his chest. "It must have been a terrible battle."

"All battles are terrible. Ironically, I was not hurt on the field, but after I was captured. The Italian guard, Edwardo, learned I was part Romany and he used his sword to teach me a lesson. To this day, I am unsure of the lesson, but apparently he preferred my English part and wanted to use my Romany part as an example to not be born."

Her gasp caught in her throat.

Stefan kissed her temples. "I managed to strike a few blows to his face before I was chained. Mayhap that was why Edwardo did not like me. In the end, we agreed on a truce that benefitted us both. I persuaded him to allow me to escape from prison, knowing King Henry would bestow on me a title and lands for fighting in the battle. I would reward Edwardo with a portion of my wealth. I made good on my agreement. Edwardo now works for me."

She frowned. "Doing what, exactly?"

"At present, he is escorting a certain Sir Thomas Windchoice to the Spanish border."

She traced each scar on his chest. "You disappeared for so long. When the third year came and went my uncle secured an agreement with Sir Thomas. I tried to send word to you, but you never responded. Were you in prison?"

"Aye. When I finally escaped with Edwardo's help, I returned posthaste to Yorkshire but you were gone. No one, not even your sister, would tell me where you went."

"Most likely she felt ashamed and fearful for her own safety."

"The months I rotted in that wretched filth of a jail, I thought of you. Our memories of you and me kept me alive."

Catherine bent her head and slid her lips along each pale silver slash, as if she could take away all the pain he'd suffered. She couldn't imagine it, of course, but she could imagine that some pain never went away. Stefan had had grand dreams, but with grand dreams came enormous regrets.

Her lips traveled lower down the line of hair on his stomach.

All the muscles in his body bunched. He stilled and raised her face to his. "If you continue to kiss me like that, you will drive me mad."

She smiled. "'Tis exactly my intention."

He gave a quiet laugh and quickly pulled off his boots.

She was prepared for the sight of his muscular legs. She wasn't prepared for the sight of his mangled right foot.

Her world seemed to stop.

"Let me explain," he began.

Her gaze was fixed to his foot, her body motionless. Her earlier, cruel jibes about his fancy life raced through her mind.

"Your limp," she said quietly. "'Tis not caused by gout."

"Edwardo tore my foot as well as my chest and it never healed properly."

"And you forgave this man?

"Forgiveness is a powerful thing. It begins within ourselves." Stefan closed his eyes. How could he explain the hours of pondering and prayer he spent before coming to his decision not to blame Edwardo for his ignorance against the Rom?

"You are a much stronger man than I ever imagined," she said.

"Adversity gave me strength. Eventually, Edwardo and I developed a respect for each other, a commonality borne of poverty and war. When I left the prison, I saw a barber surgeon, but there was little to be done except use leeches on my leg. I would have tried anything, as long as I was able to get back to you. After my planned escape, I endured moments when I feared you might not accept a man less than whole."

She sprinkled kisses across his handsome face. "Let me help you heal."

He caught her lips in a hard kiss. "Make no mistake, Catherine, 'tis not an invitation I will turn down a second time. I am no longer the green lad you once knew."

* * *

SHE SHOOK HER HEAD. "Stefan, I am so sorry for your terrible wounds."

He wrapped his arms around her. "No pity, only a promise that we will never lose each other again."

"You never lost me, because I never stopped loving you."

Desire swept across his face like a shadow.

He gathered her close. "Catherine, I missed you so much."

They slept for a while. They must have. A minute, an hour later, she couldn't be sure, as she hovered somewhere between dreams and awareness. She opened her eyes and surveyed her small, shabby chamber. The fire in the fireplace had burned out. Her bed was cold. Stefan must have awakened, for she heard his boots tapping against the stone floor.

He'd return in a moment. He had vowed he'd never lose her.

She closed her eyes. All was well.

CHAPTER 8

*W*hen next Catherine opened her eyes, twilight had darkened her chamber. She stirred, dragging herself from sleep before looking around the room.

The chamber was still chilly.

The chamber was still empty.

She bolted awake. He'd left her. Again. Her body quaked. Tears threatened.

Nay, she refused to let them fall.

She yanked back the bedcovers and sprang to her feet.

"Where are you going?" Stefan asked from the doorway. He strode to the fireplace with a bundle of wood and knelt near the grate.

"I thought you were gone," she said by way of an answer, but her tone was unsteady. She shook her head. Ridiculous. He vowed never to lose her. She needed to trust his word.

"I left to gather more wood," he said.

She tried again, her voice steadier. "Good, because this chamber is always cold and drafty. Are you hungry?"

His grin was wicked. "Only for you, darling, and only if you serve gingerbread."

She laughed aloud as he strode to her. In the refuge of his arms, she rested her cheek against his chest, hearing the rhythmic thumping of his heart.

She was safe. She was secure.

"We shall head to Yorkshire come the morrow," he said.

Absently, she glided her hands in circles on his chest. "Bess will be thrilled when she hears I shall be leaving. She is not at all fond of me."

"Bess does not fancy anyone. Especially an astute woman like you who keeps the Bankside ledgers accurate."

Her hands stopped. She gazed into Stefan's eyes. He seemed to be attempting to keep his features solemn, but the laugh lines around his eyes deepened.

"Something more that you want to tell me?" she asked.

"Bess fancies coin, not people. She has filched from the brothel's coffers every day for years. Apparently, she has been greedier than usual of late."

"Did your jaunt to get more wood for the fireplace also include a visit to Bess?"

"Before I left the brothel the other day, I took the liberty of going through the ledgers and confronted her. When I threatened to expose her stealing, she admitted her guilt. Tonight, we decided on a satisfactory agreement."

Catherine attempted not to smile, but couldn't help it when she saw the grin threatening to overtake Stefan's face.

"With the money Bess accumulated over the years," he continued, "she is purchasing the brothel from Thomas Windchoice. Bess is the new owner of Hollands Leaguer."

"So, she is buying the property with the money she stole from Sir Thomas?"

Stefan still was grinning. "There are many ways to describe the purchase, but yours is the most accurate."

"She can have the miserable place, along with the horrid memories," Catherine murmured.

Stefan tightened his arms around her, as if he were trying to soak up all the shame she had endured.

"Come the morrow, my coach shall be waiting, along with my servants and footmen and outriders. We shall ride to my country estate in Aylsham."

She swallowed. "You wish me to reside at your estate as your mistress?"

"As my wife," he clarified. "Following a proper wedding, you shall take your place beside me where you belong. And your sister will be well provided for."

She hesitated and then blurted. "I need to confess something."

"Should I be alarmed?"

She withdrew from his grasp and lit the candle on her bureau. Then she turned back to him and waited.

"Confession time?" he prompted.

"I never told you how much I love you, and I... I wanted you to know." Her voice shook with an affection she didn't try to hide.

He stroked his thumbs under her eyes to catch her tears. "I love you more."

"Stefan?"

"Mmm?"

"How did you manage to banish Sir Thomas from England, sell the brothel to Bess, and arrange for my sister's care, all in the few days since you found me?"

He smiled and captured her lips in one long kiss. When he lifted his mouth, the young, carefree lad she remembered from years past seemed to take the older Stefan's place.

"I will take half the credit," he said. "Let's attribute the other half to Gypsy magic."

THE END

A NOTE FROM JOSIE

Dear Friends,

Thank you for spending time with Catherine and her story. I have been fascinated by the Tudor and Regency eras since I was a girl.

The candlelit drawing rooms, the careful words exchanged between a man and a woman who dared not say too much, two people standing close and feeling everything they could not speak aloud. I never grow tired of it.

If Catherine's story stayed with you the way it stayed with me, I would be grateful if you shared an honest review here.

Seeking Catherine is available in ebook, paperback, Large Print paperback, Hardcover, and an incredible audiobook read by my gifted British voice actress whose accent makes every scene feel as though you are standing in a Regency parlor yourself.

I'd love to meet you in person someday, but in the meantime, all I can offer is a sincere and grateful thank you. Without your support, my books would not be possible.

As I write my next sweet or inspirational romance,

remember this: Have you ever tried something you were afraid to try because it mattered so much to you? I did, when I started writing. Take the chance, and just do something you love.

With gratitude,
Josie Riviera
P.S. My Spotify Playlist for Seeking Catherine is here.

RECIPE FOR TUDOR GINGERBREAD

Ingredients

• 14 slices of crumbed, stale brown bread with crusts removed

• 1 small jar of honey

Scant amounts of ground black pepper, nutmeg, ground star anise, and ginger.

In small saucepan, warm honey and do not let it boil.

In bowl, combine half of the breadcrumbs, honey, and spices. Add more breadcrumbs until absorbed.

Press in 8 inch cake tin. Let stand at room temperature for 1 day.

Enjoy!

BONUS: SNEAK PEEK AT SEEKING FORTUNE (A REGENCY INSPIRATIONAL ROMANCE) PREVIEW

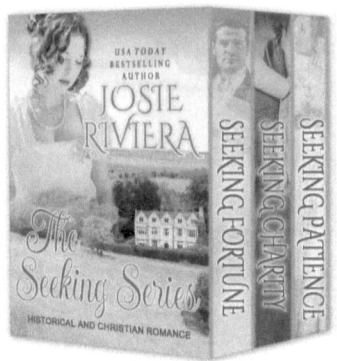

*C*hapter One Excerpt from Seeking Fortune, the first book in
The Seeking Series

Si khohaimo may patshivalo sar o tshatshim.

> There are lies more believable than the truth.
> Old Romany saying

ENGLAND 1811

"BURY ME STANDING, for I have been on my knees all my life."

Valentina Rupa bowed her head to hear her beloved mother's last words, to see the twitch of her eyes beneath her eyelids, the rise and fall of her chest beneath the thin blankets.

Her mother's breath faded, already settling into the bleak night, already gone.

Unearthly quiet filled their makeshift canopy. The dwindling light from the nearby campfires of their Romany tribe seeped through the canvas.

"*Daj.* Mother ... don't stop speaking." Tears blinded Valentina's eyes, defeated her voice. She focused on her mother's lips, willing her to speak once more. What good did it do to be a *drabardi*, a powerful fortune-teller and healer if she couldn't save her own mother?

Valentina's younger sister, Yolanda, stood beside her. Yolanda coughed violently, then wheezed.

"Please, Daj, it's not your time." Yolanda's hoarse voice faded to a whisper. "Her lips, she's breathing ..."

"Nay, it's the north wind." Valentina peered at the oak tree branches bending against a biting gust, threatening collapse their crude canopy. Wagon wheels creaked, groaning into the dirt, familiar sounds, yet so distant. Their mother had lived her entire life in the caravan, traveling from village to village. There was no other way for her. Only the way of the Romany.

The air hung thick and heavy, warning of a hailstorm, stinging Valentina's damp cheeks. She didn't care, didn't bother to wipe them. She hated the weakness of crying. Crying meant loss and loneliness and defeat.

She glanced at Yolanda, noting her ashen face, the stoop of her slight shoulders. "Try to rest for a while."

"I'm not tired." Yolanda rubbed her temples. "Now that both Mother and Father are dead, we're orphans."

"I'll not abandon you." Valentina choked back her fears and crushing uncertainties. She was the older sister. She always took care of Yolanda.

With shaking fingers, she tucked the threadbare blankets around their mother's feeble body, smoothed the wrinkled fabric, and folded the ends back. Neatly, the way her mother liked it done. Tucked, smoothed, folded. Tucked, smoothed, folded.

"Daj, you starved yourself so we could eat. We'd have found the food we needed somehow." Her hands glided purposefully. "Why do the English treat the Rom as if we're animals?"

"Because this is the land of the English," Yolanda said. "They make their own rules."

Long shivers rippled through Valentina's body, a cadence of trepidation and doubt. In a single, deliberate breath, she blew them out.

The friends who'd discreetly stayed out of the way melted in now, coming from their wagons to gather around the deathbed. The sad cries of the caravan penetrated the dusk. Purple-lipped, the elderly, ragged men and women huddled together, stamping their feet to keep away the chill.

With the sleeve of her frayed cotton gown, Valentina wiped her eyes. Her hands were still wet from retrieving water from the river. She'd used the water to bathe her mother, an ironic Romany custom relying on her mother's willingness to go to her death.

Yolanda helped Valentina gather their mother's personal belongings and carried them to the campfire. The flames rose against the night sky and consumed the remnants of their mother's life—a well-worn apron, a silky fringed sash. Their people burned most possessions of the dead, believing the possessions were unclean and defiled the living.

Valentina skimmed her index finger across her mother's double-edged dagger and accidentally drew blood. Grimacing, she licked her finger. She didn't have the heart to destroy the weapon, so she thrust the dagger into its sheath and tied it on a cord along her gown's seam.

Then she slid her palm across the last treasure, her mother's yellow scarf, her *diklo*. Bringing it to her face, Valentina closed her eyes and inhaled. The scent of oak and jasmine, exotic and mysterious, flooded through her. She remembered her mother jauntily tying the diklo around her greying hair each morning.

Valentina knew she was supposed to take one small token before burial, although she took two. She'd never been one to obey rules. She folded the yellow scarf into a perfect triangle and tied it loosely around her throat. It didn't match her faded scarlet gown, and that didn't matter.

Nothing mattered now except her sister.

Yolanda's pretty, round face contorted in grief as she placed small multicolored stones around their mother's body. Valentina inserted pearls in her mother's nose to keep out all wickedness. Her hands wavered, and she avoided touching the body for fear of contamination.

Inhaling the fragrance of a drop of frankincense, she smoothed the spicy golden oil along her arms to protect herself against evil spirits. A shadow of skepticism crossed her soul, and her hands stopped. Maybe spirits didn't exist at all. They certainly demanded endless rituals, and in return granted … nothing. Glancing around at the eerie silhouettes dancing in the firelight, she dabbed a few more drops of oil on her wrists, just in case.

The men of their tribe had moved to sit in the grassy clearing on the forest's edge, the scent of sweet blackberry brandy filling the brisk October air. They'd stolen it from an unsuspecting Englishman in town. Several grizzled dogs lay listless at their feet.

Luca, the caravan's young leader, was the only man who stood. His baggy green pants were fitted at the ankle and billowed in the wind. He mourned Valentina and Yolanda's mother in a plaintive cadence and guided the elders in solemn chants. Although all the other young men had gone off in search of food and never returned, Luca hadn't deserted the tribe.

"I'll get more hot water, Yolanda, before we prepare for Daj's burial." Valentina retrieved her wool cloak and then hoisted a pot of water off of a smoky campfire. With her free hand, she brushed a strand of hair behind her ear, longing for a warm bath. However, custom prevented her from washing until after her mother's burial.

She made her way past the lamenters to the small tent the women shared. An afternoon rain had washed soggy leaves over the ground. One of the dogs lifted its head and sniffed, the thick fur around its neck bristling. A sudden crackle— somewhere a tree branch snapped.

Her senses sharpened. The last few nights she'd dozed while nursing her mother and had dreamed about a man. A rich man. A powerful man.

Scanning the dense woods, she sensed someone was watching. She had the gift of second sight, her mother had said, but Valentina shook the thought away. Besides, her tribe was far too secluded to be found.

*** End of excerpt *Seeking Fortune* by Josie Riviera
Copyright © 2018 Josie Riviera
***

READ the rest of Seeking Fortune, an inspirational Regency romance.

And, find out why readers are falling in love with The Seeking Series. These are sweet, inspirational Christian romances.

Each book tells the story of a Romany hero or heroine who risks the heart for love, faith, and the life they were always meant to live.

Valentina and James wait for you in Seeking Fortune, Daniel and Charity in Seeking Charity, Luca and Patience in Seeking Patience, and Nash and Rachel in Seeking Rachel.

Or save and indulge all at once with THE SEEKING SERIES bundle. Pick up your copy today! Available in ebook, paperback, audiobook, Hardcover, and Large Print Paperback.

ABOUT THE AUTHOR

USA TODAY bestselling author, Josie Riviera, writes Historical, Inspirational, and Sweet Romances. She lives in the Charlotte, NC, area with her wonderfully supportive husband. They share their home with an adorable shih tzu, who constantly needs grooming, and live in an old house forever needing renovations.

To receive my Newsletter and your free sweet romance novella ebook as a thank you gift, sign up Here.

Also, become a member of my Read and Review VIP Facebook group for exclusive giveaways and ARCs.

You'll get sneak peeks at my newest books, as well as content not found anywhere else.

To connect with Josie, visit her website and sign up for her newsletter. As a thank-you, she'll send you a free sweet romance novella.
josieriviera.com/

PRAISE AND AWARDS

USA TODAY bestselling author

Top 13 Amazon Bestseller Ancient World Historical Romance

Top 10 Amazon Bestseller Medieval Historical Romance

5 STAR READER REVIEWS: SEEKING CATHERINE

"I find stories which explore cultural differences interesting and this writer does an excellent job. Opposites attract in this novel for an interesting plot."- Amazon Reviewer

"I loved this. What a terrific escape. I got into it and had a hard time stopping! I needed that, thanks!"- Amazon Reviewer

"What woman could ever read this book and. Not be waiting impatiently for their true love to find them. It would and could be their dream come true.

This is well written as Katherine was found by her one true love and she was happy to see him." - Amazon Reviewer

"I happen to love part-Gypsy heroes and heroines who will do whatever it takes to survive--to my delight, Seeking Catherine has both. Seeking Cathrine is an enjoyable Novella set in Tudor England, with sparkling banter and emotional resonance. Looking forward to Josie Riviera's next!" - Amazon Reviewer

ACKNOWLEDGMENTS

An appreciative thank you to my patient husband, Dave, and our three wonderful children.

ALSO BY JOSIE RIVIERA

Seeking Patience

Seeking Catherine (always Free!)

Seeking Fortune

Seeking Charity

Seeking Rachel

The Seeking Series

Oh Danny Boy

I Love You More

A Snowy White Christmas

A Portuguese Christmas

Holiday Hearts Book Bundle Volume One

Holiday Hearts Book Bundle Volume Two

Holiday Hearts Book Bundle Volume Three

Holiday Hearts Book Bundle Volume Four

Holiday Hearts Book Bundle Volume Five

Candleglow and Mistletoe

Maeve (Perfect Match)

A Love Song To Cherish

A Christmas To Cherish

A Valentine To Cherish

A Christmas Puppy To Cherish

A Homecoming To Cherish

A Summer To Cherish

Romance Stories To Cherish

Romance Stories To Cherish Volume Two

Cherished Hearts Six Book Volume

Aloha To Love

Sweet Peppermint Kisses

Valentine Hearts Boxed Set

1-800-CUPID

1-800-CHRISTMAS

1-800-IRELAND

1-800-SUMMER

1-800-NEW YEAR

The 1-800-Series Sweet Contemporary Romance Bundle

Irish Hearts Sweet Romance Bundle

Holly's Gift

A Chocolate-Box Christmas

A Chocolate-Box New Years

A Chocolate-Box Valentine

A Chocolate-Box Summer Breeze

A Chocolate-Box Christmas Wish

A Chocolate-Box Irish Wedding

Chocolate-Box Hearts

Chocolate-Box Hearts Volume Two

Chocolate-Box Double Hearts

Recipes From The Heart

Leading Hearts

New Year Hearts

SENIOR HEARTS

Summer Hearts

Christmas in the Air (1-800-Book)

A Very Christian Christmas

The 1-800-Series Volume Two

The 1-800-Series Complete

Christmas Tails of the Heart

Cocoa's Christmas Love

Pawfect Christmas Hearts

Pink Coral Island

Whispers of Love in Sweetwater Springs

Whispers of Maple Memories in Sweetwater Springs

Whispers of Holiday Magic in Sweetwater Springs

Whispers of Sweetwater Springs

A Harvest of Miracles

A Winter Promise

A Season Out of Time

Hearts and Horseshoes

Wishes and Wildflowers

1-800-CUPIDON (French Edition)

1-800-CUPDO (Spanish Edition)

1-800-AMOR (German Edition)

Most books are available in ebook, audiobook, paperback, Large Print paperback and Hardcover.

Many are FREE on Kindle Unlimited!

A GIFT FOR YOU

To keep up on newly released ebooks, paperbacks, Large Print Paperbacks, audiobooks, as well as exclusive sales, sign up for Josie's Newsletter today.

As a thank you, I'll send you a Free PDF ... The Beauty Of ...

Josie's Newsletter

Did you know that according to a Yale University study, people who read books live longer?